5-minute
GOODNIGHT STORIES

DERRYDALE BOOKS
New York

Contents

	page
The birthday present	8
A tale of ancient times	10
The sleepy little sandman	12
Susan in the department store	14
The ladybird and the bee	16
Whirlygig's toothache	18
THE OAKDALE SCHOOL FOR BUNNIES	21
Summer holidays	22
Beginning of term	24
In the classroom	26
Autumn in Oakdale	28
Winter has arrived	32
Snow holidays	34
Messengers of spring	36
Easter	38
Time for school reports!	40
The nutcracker	41
Bernie's garden	44
Giddy the goat	46
Melchior and Balthasar	48
The rhino and the bird	50
Polly's roller-skates	52
The chatterbox	54
THE SCHOOL FOR PIXIES	56
The pixie caps	57
The mouse	58
The race	61
On the way to school	63
Late!	65
Good friends	67
Gymnastics	69
At home	71
Dreams	73
Last day at school	75
Tit for tat	76
Conversations in the hall	78
In the woods	80
The little sister	82
Arthur the garden gnome	84
The impossible crocodile	86
The little birch tree	88
The grasshopper	90
The impatient raindrop	92
Cherries as big as pumpkins	94
The little hen that went exploring	96

	page
Nina's Dream House	98
The Mole and the Anemone	100
Nick at the dentist	102
Rudie the rabbit	104
The story of Blowy	106
Happiness	108
The bird and the cactus	110
The old-fashioned balloons	112
Judy and the pea	114
Jack is not hungry	116
The curious mouse	118
The flying elephant	120
Paul and the pedestrian crossing	122
The woodworm	124
The little red hat	126
Robin's disturbing night	128
Seeds in the ears	130
Tommy at the Post Office	132
Patrick the runaway	134
Of gnomes and people	136
The absent-minded pixie	138
Dachsie's secret	140
The wooden round-about	143
The rhubarb leaf	146
The polar bear and the raccoon	149
Cathy's long journey	152
CHRISTMAS IN STORYLAND	155
The Christmas Mail	156
The Christmas Angels	158
On the way to the gnomes' house	160
Visiting the gnomes	162
At work	166
Final preparations	168
It's Christmas	170
The surprise	172
The crooked little fir tree	175
CHRISTMAS WITH THE ANGELS	177
Look at the time!	177
George	180
Michael in the cradle	182
A house full of wishes	184
Don't wish for too much!	186
Back in heaven	188
View through the peephole	190
Christmas at the forester's house	192
Well done!	195

The birthday present

When Andy woke up the sun was already shining into his room. All was quiet, only a few birds were chirping in the garden.

The little boy sat up. It was his birthday! Swiftly he slid out of bed and looked for his slippers.

The presents! Mummy always hid them. Andy set about finding them. He ran through all the rooms but he couldn't find a present anywhere.

Then Andy heard something at the front door. He opened the door slightly. A little kitten sat on the doorstep and mewed quietly. Slowly it came through the door and walked towards Andy. Then it tried to climb up to him. Andy took the kitten in his arms and hugged it carefully. It purred happily and snuggled deeper into his arms. Feeling very excited, Andy ran to his parents with the kitten.

"Mummy, Daddy!" he cried happily. "Thank you, thank you! I've never had such a nice present before!" His parents looked puzzled, as Andy didn't get the kitten from them!

They bought a scooter with rubber tyres, which Andy had wanted for a long time. It was in the garden under the apple tree.

Andy enjoyed the best birthday of his life. He could keep the kitten and he was given a scooter as well. But where did the kitten come from? It must have known it was Andy's birthday and sat on the doorstep — as a present.

A tale of ancient times

A little stream wound through the green meadows. At its banks stood tall, ancient willows, poplars and birch trees. Its water was bright and clear; you could watch the trout swimming. A little bird called Peep had his nest in one of the ancient willows. He was sitting on a branch when a strong smell of petrol went up his nose. It startled him because he didn't usually get the smell of petrol here.

And what was that noise? A whole convoy of trucks and diggers was pushing across the meadow. The new motorway was being built here. The little stream had to be diverted through underground pipes. Of course the willows, birch trees and poplars could not remain on the motorway. So they had to be cut down. The green meadow had to make way for a straight, grey covering of asphalt. Soon nothing was left of the pretty country scenery.

The ancient willow, where Peep once lived, had gone. So he made his nest in the archway of the concrete bridge. He had to adjust to a lot of new things. He had to get used to the noise, too. But he missed the branches of trees most of all. Where should he sit when he wanted to sing in the morning?

As time went by, Peep told his children of the clear stream, the willows and poplars. Also of the nest in the willow tree which he loved so much.

And to his children it seemed that he was telling a tale of ancient times. . . .

The sleepy little sandman

Darkness grew slowly. The birds were already asleep in their nests and the children had gone to bed. That's the time the little sandman was at his busiest. With his little bag of sleeping sand he went from house to house and sprinkled tiny specks of sand into the children's eyes.

All the children were asleep, and the little sandman wearily made his way home. Outside the town he thought, "I must just check how much sand I've got left in my little bag!" But as soon as he untied the bag he started to sneeze, "atchoo! atchoo!" and so much sand got into his eyes that he yawned heartily and fell asleep straight away. He slept and slept — through the night and the whole of the following day. And in the evening the little sandman was still asleep.

Then a little pixie found him. He shook and shook him but the little sandman didn't move. "What shall I do?" cried the pixie. "Who will sprinkle sleeping sand into the children's eyes?"

But then he had a good idea. He asked the birds which were sitting on their nests by now, for help. Each bird took as much sand into its beak as it could carry and flew to a house where children lived. The children lay in bed still awake, of course. But as soon as the birds sprinkled the sleeping sand around, the children fell asleep.

That's why to this day, all children go to sleep before the birds.

Susan in the department store

Susan went into the big department store with her mother. She would have loved to spend the whole day there. Her mother held Susan's hand firmly so she wouldn't get lost.

The escalator looked great fun to Susan. She watched how the other people were doing it. One person after another quickly stood on a step and waited until that step reached the top. It didn't seem too difficult, so while her mother was talking to the sales lady, Susan thought she'd try it herself.

She travelled up on the escalator through the whole store until she arrived at the toy department. There, however, she forgot the escalator. Susan went from shelf to shelf looking at all the wonderful toys and dolls. But suddenly she remembered her mother. How could she find her again in this big department store?

Susan felt frightened and started to cry. There were lots of people there but none of them was her mother. "Why are you crying?" a young sales lady asked her. "I don't know where my Mummy is," sobbed Susan. Then a message went over the loudspeakers, "Attention! Attention! Little Susan is upstairs in the toy department and is looking for her Mummy." Her mother heard this and rushed up to the toy department. Susan ran to her. "Mummy, I'm so glad you're here. I will never run away again!" she sobbed.

The ladybird and the bee

The little ladybird had been flying from flower to flower all day in the sunshine. In the afternoon it was busy chasing away those ugly greenflies from the roses in the garden. "Bzzz" and a little bee came visiting the rose bush. "Are you here for the greenflies, too?" asked the ladybird, but the bee buzzed angrily with its wings and snarled,

"What should I do with greenflies? I take the pollen from the roses and put it in the little bags on my legs. I also collect nectar. Then I fly back to my beehive where we make honey from the nectar."

"How wonderful," sighed the ladybird. "Who else lives with you in the beehive?"

"My queen and many, many other bees," replied the bee and buzzed to the next flower. The ladybird stayed behind and was a little sad.

Then it noticed that the big glowing sun had gone from the sky and the earth was getting darker. It was time to find a place for the night.

What was that? A bright light, almost as bright as the sun, was shining in the direction of the ladybird. Quickly it flew towards the light. Where do you think it landed? It came straight through the window and landed on my table lamp. And that's where it told me its story!

Whirlygig's toothache

What a beautiful morning it was! The bright sunlight was shining through the window when Whirlygig the gnome woke up. "Good morning, lazybones," cried the sun. "Time to get up!"

But Whirlygig would much rather snuggle deeper under the blankets. He couldn't sleep all night because of toothache. "Oh dear, Oh dear," he cried. "My tooth hurts so much!"

It was the same tooth the gnome dentist had said for a long time should be taken out. "Oh dear! If I had only gone to the dentist earlier." He turned onto his other side but the tooth still hurt. In the end he couldn't bear to be in bed any longer. He got up and had a wash. But all the time he had to lay his hand on his painful cheek. That seemed to help a little.

Later Whirlygig sat on the bench in front of his house. He didn't know what to do. He'd tied a large headscarf round his head and held his cheek. "You're looking very sad today, Whirlygig," said the bluebell sympathetically. "You usually laugh and sing happily."

"Oh, I don't feel much like laughing today," said the gnome and a big tear ran down his face. "I've got such bad toothache, but I'm even more afraid to go to the dentist."

Gently the bluebell swayed in the wind and said, "But Whirlygig, only the dentist can help you, and afterwards everything will be much more fun." But still Whirlygig couldn't find the courage to go to the dentist. Nothing was fun anymore. While the other gnomes were having fun and playing he sat sadly on his bench. But eventually he said to the bluebell, "There is no other way — I must go to the dentist after all!"

"Don't be afraid, you'll soon be able to laugh again," said the bluebell.

Trembling with fear he set off to go to the dentist. To his surprise he didn't feel a thing when the dentist pulled out the bad tooth and at last the toothache had gone. And Whirlygig wasn't afraid of the dentist anymore, either.

At last he could go and laugh and play with the other gnomes again.

THE OAKDALE SCHOOL FOR BUNNIES

Summer holidays

At last the holidays have arrived! School has finished and we put away the books for a few weeks. Holidays are for playing! The bunnies, too, look forward to school holidays. There they are no different from children. At last they can play outside all day long or go to the mountains or the seaside with their parents.

No bunny thinks of learning tables in the holidays but some bunnies like to read a really good book. But most of all the bunnies like playing ball. Then they can run about as much as they like and also prove how clever they are. There are usually some onlookers around to cheer the players. That really sets the game going!

It's wonderful to chase over the meadows. The bunnies try to catch each other or butterflies.

Occasionally they calm down a bit and study plants and beetles, the way they learned in school. There is always something new to discover. In a few days school will start again. Bunnies, like human children, are sad that they will now have less time to play. But they also look forward to the start of school as they will be able to see their friends again. "I'll tell Hop all about my holidays," says Skip happily.

Beginning of term

It's time to get out the old school satchels or to buy new ones. It is a little hard for the bunnies to collect together all the books. Their parents buy new pens and exercise books, paint brushes and erasers, sometimes even fountain pens and felt tips. And now they are ready!

No more sleeping in! They all have to be at school early. Bunny mums and dads hold the paws of new pupils. They have bags of sweets for playtime. They are quite excited. A new boy looks pleadingly at his mother, as if to say, "Don't leave me and come with me."
A big bunny says to his little brother, "Don't be worried about school. Nobody is going to eat you! Look how many bunnies are running to school happily." And with that he ran off to greet his school friends. "Which class are we in?" Skip asked his friend. And the most important question, of course, "which teacher will we have this term?"

In the classroom

At last the bunnies are taken to their classrooms. Skip and his friend want to sit together like they did last term. Naturally today the bunnies can't keep still, they want to chatter and whisper. Skip's friend Hop has a lot to tell, too. Then the teacher asked each bunny about their school holidays. That way the bunnies don't realize that the lesson has already begun.

After a little while the lessons start seriously. For the whole morning the bunnies sit in class and work hard. The teacher tells the pupils about the letter S. But today the bunnies are noisy and pay no attention. "If you don't stop chattering, you will never learn anything," says the teacher. The bunnies pay attention again because they do want to learn.

The teacher is pleased with his pupils. They have already learned to write, read, count, draw and paint. And they also enjoy singing. They're not very good but they enjoy it. And that's the main thing!

The bunnies listen most carefully during the nature lesson. They learn about trees and plants, carrots and cabbages, other animals and different seasons. It's important for the young bunnies to know all these things.

Autumn in Oakdale

Slowly autumn is coming. The days become shorter and colder. In the autumn, leaves turn into different colours, yellow, gold, orange, brown, rust and red. The trees look beautiful. One day Skip's teacher asks the bunnies to collect leaves for the art lesson. What are they going to do with them? They all bring a handful of very pretty leaves and spread them out on their desks. They stick the leaves on to sheets of paper and make beautiful pictures.

But the bunnies don't spend all the autumn in the classroom. They roam through the woods and meadows, fly kites and they play games. Several bunnies collect a pile of leaves and then they take turns at falling into the pile. Great fun! And it makes a lovely rustling noise, too.

During break time the bunnies enjoy shuffling through the thick carpet of leaves. Some bunnies gather lots of leaves and throw them at each other. That was fun for a few days but then they stopped. It's not such fun having their ears scrubbed every day!

Winter has arrived

The bunnies like going to school. They go every day, even in the wet and foggy weather of November or the cold, snow and ice of December. The school building is covered in snow and is hidden among the old oak trees. But the bunnies don't mind the cold and snow of the winter. They dress in warmer clothes and wear thick scarves around their necks. And in the classroom a little stove warms the room. After throwing snowballs at each other the bunnies run to the little stove to warm their paws. It is hard to write with frozen paws!

But in the next playtime they run outside again and throw snowballs at each other. When they run about a lot the bunnies get really warm. But they are careful because they know it's very easy to get hurt if they throw a snowball in someone's face.

The teacher has forbidden them to throw snowballs but as soon as one bunny starts everyone forgets what the teacher has said, and a new snowball fight is on the way. Suddenly the teacher comes out and some bunnies pretend they haven't joined in the fight. The teacher knows that they have been playing with snowballs though, because the bunnies still have snow on their paws!

Snow holidays

It is the middle of January and a terrible snowstorm starts. The wind blows the snow through the trees and the animals look for shelter or stay in their homes. Nobody wants to make the first step in the deep snow. When the storm is over the freezing snow creaks and the lakes and rivers are covered with a thick layer of ice. It is bitterly cold. Of course during this weather the school house remains closed and the bunnies can stay home. A few extra holidays are always welcome! The bunnies stick their paws and noses deep under the blankets and have a good lie-in in the mornings. And mother does not call, "Get up you bunnies, it's late."

Skip, Hop and Swift really enjoy days like these. "We really must have a rest," declares Swift. "When we go back to school we have to work really hard to get good school reports!" Mother just nods and laughs. They are quite nice bunnies, really!

The bunnies decide they must make the most of the unexpected holiday. They read their books and play with their toys all day long. They have to stay out of their mother's way and keep their bedroom tidy, too!

Messengers of spring

Soon the warm sun shines through the window, the icicles melt from the roof and the snowman in front of the house becomes smaller and smaller. By now the bunnies just can't bear to stay indoors any longer.

Carefully they test the spring air with their little noses and then with a big leap they hop outside. The sound of their laughter and shouting can be heard for miles. Soon all the bunnies from Skip's class are gathered together at school again. Swift sees the first messenger of spring in the snow, a little snowdrop. "Look here," he shouts to the others and carefully he picks it to show to the teacher. The bunnies pay attention and work hard for a while. But when the sun shines into the classroom they don't want to sit indoors any longer. They ask the teacher if they can have the lessons outside as it's spring time.

The bunnies are very surprised when the teacher agrees and says, "I had planned to talk about spring arriving . We will go for a long walk tomorrow." The whole class squeals with delight. The bunnies are really excited and look forward to their day out in the sunshine and fresh air.

Easter

While the little bunnies are busy learning about nature with their teacher, the adults have a lot to do. Soon it will be Easter and a lot of eggs have to be bought and painted.

The bunnies look forward to Easter and talk about nothing else for weeks. They are working out where to hide the eggs this year so that the baby bunnies will have a lot of fun finding them. Skip has some good ideas again. Hop claps his paws with delight when he hears where the baby bunnies will have to look for the eggs. He laughs and jumps from one leg onto the other. But they decide that Swift's idea is best. He wants to hide some eggs in Peter's rabbit hutch. "He'll be surprised!" they cry. Everybody laughs at the joke. The girl bunnies try to make the Easter nests as pretty as possible. "I will put red and yellow eggs under the blue flowers. That will look very pretty," says Fluffy. Her friend Fifi agrees and she puts a little basket under the pussy willows. "Will a purple egg go with a pink one?" asks Fifi.

The bunnies all agree that the eggs look very pretty. They are pleased with their hard work.

At last Easter arrives.

Time for school reports

Helping with the Easter preparations is also a kind of school test for the bunnies. They have to show that they can read and count. And that will be important for the school reports. On Easter morning Skip and his friends set off with the eggs. There are three baby bunnies living in the house next door. Swift says, "Three times five is fifteen," and quickly the bunnies run through the garden to hide that many eggs. They leave five eggs for each bunny at every house until they have hidden them all.

Skip is proud and says, "Hooray! We've counted correctly." That is very important. What would happen if we left only nine eggs for two baby bunnies. Someone would be very disappointed!

After Easter each bunny takes home a school report. Skip and his brothers are very pleased, they all had good marks. Their parents will be very happy.

"I hope we have a juicy carrot each," says Swift to his brother. Of course their mother and father know what the bunnies like best and these good school reports must be celebrated! The bunnies' mother and father are really pleased with their children for such good reports and they give them a nice big carrot each.

The Nutcracker

Steven's Grandma had a nutcracker — a beautiful wooden nutcracker with a white beard and a hat on its head, decorated with a few little flowers. It stood on top of the bookshelf in the living room. "Grandma, may I play with the nutcracker!" Steven asked every time he visited his Grandma. Patsy, the little girl next door, often played with it, too. Grandma took the wooden man from the shelf and said, "Here you are, but don't break it." Steven put a nut into the nutcracker's mouth and worked the lever on its back. With a loud crack the nut shell broke open. "Well done, little nutcracker!" said Steven.

One day, however, Steven put the nutcracker back in its place and was very quiet. Grandma tried in vain to cheer him up. And when his mother arrived to pick him up he was quite relieved. Next day Grandma visited Steven. He was not as pleased as usual to see her. He didn't laugh much and Grandma was rather worried, "What's the matter with the boy?" she asked. "Well, you know, Steven is very unhappy. Yesterday he broke off the little flowers from the nutcracker's hat. You specially said not to break it," Steven's mother explained.

Grandma began to laugh and shook her head. "But those little flowers were already broken. Little Patsy from next door did that the last time she played with the nutcracker," she said. She went into Steven's room. The little boy was sitting on the floor and looked worried. "Steven," she said, and patted him on the head gently, "you don't need to be sad any more. It wasn't you that broke the flowers on the nutcraker's hat. It was little Patsy." Steven hugged his Grandma and said, "I was so afraid, I didn't sleep all night."

"Silly boy!" Grandma said, and gave him a big cuddle. "You should have told me about the nutcracker straight away and you would have saved yourself a lot of worry!"

Bernie's garden

Bernie's father had let him use the flowerbed under the lilac trees. "I will plant radishes in my garden," said Bernie as he sprinkled seeds into the damp soil.

Every hour the little boy ran out to see whether they were growing yet. Yes, there really was something moving! Bernie was quite surprised. The soil was lifting slightly on one spot — and a worm crawled out. "Get off!" cried Bernie angrily. "This is my garden." He quickly picked up the worm and threw it over into another part of the garden. His mother watched her son and asked , "What are you doing!"

"It's a disgrace. There was a worm in my garden," grumbled Bernie. "It's my garden and no worm is allowed in there."

His mother was quite amused and said, "But the worm lives in your garden."

"Not any more!" replied Bernie, "I just threw him out into your garden. And if I find another one, I will throw him out, too."

"Well, well," his mother laughed, "and will you throw out the ants, beetles and grubs, too? Don't you know that the worm that you just threw out makes the soil in your garden nice and crumbly!" So Bernie put the worm back in his garden and said, "Back to Work!"

Giddy the goat

In a nursery outside town there stood a little stable next to a greenhouse. A goat with a long beard lived there. He was called Giddy and could bleat beautifully. Giddy was a nice goat. He liked to be fed by the children.

Lucy often went to the nursery with her mother to buy vegtables. She always went straight to the goat's stable. As soon as the nursery lady saw Lucy she picked out a carrot and one of those red, sweet apples. "See whether Giddy is hungry," she said. Lucy took the carrot and apple and ran to the stable as fast as she could. There the goat looked at her expectantly, bleated a 'hello', cocked his head and blinked at Lucy.

"Here you are," said the little girl, "look, what I've brought you. Would you like that?" and she offered the carrot to the goat. Giddy even liked being touched and stroked. First one ear, then the other.

When her mother called her, Lucy said, "Well, Giddy, see you again."

Giddy blinked at Lucy and watched her leave. Lucy turned round a few times and gave a wave. And they both knew that they would see each other again soon.

Melchior and Balthasar

Melchior and Balthasar were twins. Both had red hair, button noses and lots of freckles. They always wore identical clothes, went to the same school, had the same friends and, of course, got equal results at school. People could never tell them apart, they were always confused. Even their mother and father had difficulties.

When the boys were ten years old their parents asked, "What would you like for your birthday?" Without having to think about it Melchior replied, "A dog!" And Balthasar echoed, "A dog!"

Two dogs in the house? Impossible! They may be able to manage one. Melchior and Balthasar started to cry. Oh! Oh! They wanted one each. Only a very small one. Their parents were at a loss. In the end Uncle Jim said, "Why don't you give them a little Dachshund each! That's the same as having one Great Dane."

On the morning of their birthday there were two little Wire-haired Dachshunds sitting in the hall, a little frightened by the noise the delighted twins made. "What are you going to call them?" asked Uncle Jim. "Well, mine is called Melchior," giggled Melchior. "And I'm calling mine Balthasar!" cried Balthasar. And then the twins Melchior and Balthasar ran out into the garden, followed by the two little dogs Melchior and Balthasar.

The rhino and the bird

In a green meadow there lived a grey rhino. It was a little shy and a little sad because it was so grey. Every day it slowly trudged across the green meadow to a little pond for a drink. The grey rhino liked to be comfortable. He had dug out a shallow hole in the meadow for his big tummy. He was just having a little snooze when a bird arrived. It fluttered around the rhino and finally settled on his head. The rhino opened one eye and grunted, "I want to sleep!" The little bird, however, pretended not to hear. "Tweet, tweet, tweet" it sang, picked a pink flower and stuck it behind the rhino's grey ear. "You look pretty now," said the bird. "You should see yourself. You aren't quite so grey anymore!"

"Really?" said the rhino, quite unbelieving. He lifted his heavy tummy from the shallow, ran to the pond and looked into the water. True enough, he looked different. The clever bird wasn't quite satisfied yet. He picked some more flowers and decorated the rhino until he looked quite colourful.

Trudging back to his shallow, the rhino wasn't so grey anymore, not so sad and not so shy, either. The rhino and the bird sang so loudly together that they could be heard all over the meadow.

Polly's roller-skates

Polly had been given a pair of roller-skates for her birthday. Proudly she stood in front of the house to tie them on. But it wasn't very easy as the road sloped down slightly. Her friend Susy from next door came running along and cried, "Polly, come quickly! Look, what my mummy just brought me." Carelessly Polly left the roller-skates and followed Susy. Susy's dolls pram was in the garden and her doll had some new clothes which Susy and Polly wanted to try on the doll. Meanwhile one of Polly's roller-skates set off by itself. It rolled down the slope and came to a stop right in front of Rusty's kennel. The dog sniffed at the roller-skate curiously, picked it up and hid it in his kennel.

Polly was quite upset to find only one roller-skate when she returned. Susy helped her to look for the other one. But they couldn't find it. Susy had an idea. "The police use dogs to search for lost things, don't they?" she said. "Let's try that, too. Show this roller-skate to Rusty. He's very clever!" Polly liked the idea and held out the roller-skate to Rusty. "There, have a good sniff!" she said. "And please help me find the other one." Not another of these funny things, thought Rusty! Then he rummaged about in his kennel and returned with the second roller-skate, wagging his tail. "Well, can you believe it!" said Polly, "Now Rusty wants to roller-skate, too!"

The chatterbox

Most children love to speak over the telephone. Annie, a little schoolgirl with blond hair, was always first to answer the telephone when it rang. "Hello," she shouted into the receiver, still out of breath from running. Usually it was an aunt, uncle or a friend of her parents. "Oh," she complained, "It's never for me!"

Annie's friend lived next door. His name was Charlie. He was quite nice but he didn't talk much. He was the complete opposite to Annie who was always chatting.

When Annie rang Charlie to tell him how naughty that boy Terry had been to her, or why Mrs. Jenkins' cat had to go to the vet, Charlie only said, "Mmm," or, "Well." And finally he'd say, "That's it, then." When Annie asked him, "When will you give me a ring?" he would only say, "Oh, when I get a chance." Whenever he said that, Annie always felt angry. She slammed the telephone down and cried, "You're not my friend!" Annie decided that she would never ring Charlie again. But the next day she happened to see Charlie near the garden fence, and he gave her a beautiful glass marble. That was Charlie for you, he didn't say much, but he was a nice friend!

THE SCHOOL FOR PIXIES

The pixie caps

This is a story of two little pixies Tim and Turvy. Tim had red hair and Turvy had black hair and they were always up to something mischievous.

Do you know when they started to wear those tall, bright pixie caps? They started on the day they were nearly lost in the forest. They had been playing hide-and-seek among the tall grass and flowers when they got further and further away from the pixie village. They couldn't find their way back. The whole village had been out looking for them until late into the night. But without success. And if a little rabbit hadn't found them and taken them back home, this story would have had a sad ending! But the next day all the mothers got together. "What can we do so that this never happens again," they asked. Toby's mother had a good idea. "We'll make tall, different coloured pixie caps for every child."

"Yes," said the others, "that way we will be able to find our children among the tall flowers and grass!"

Of course, Tim and Turvy don't sleep with their pixie caps. They can't get lost in bed!

The sun woke them up in the morning and called, "Get up, or you'll be late for school. School starts again today!" Quickly they jumped out of bed.

The mouse

Turvy nudged his brother and giggled, "Do you remember yesterday?" "Of course," laughed Tim. Do you know why they were laughing? Well, their mother had asked the two boys to prepare their satchels for school. As Tim looked into the bag he discovered a mouse in it. It had settled in there to have a sleep. Maybe it had been in there during the entire holidays? Tim shouted into the bag "Hi!" He frightened the mouse so much that it jumped out of the bag. Where could it hide? There, a dark tube. She jumped into it quickly. But suddenly, a loud scream! Turvy and the pixies' mother looked at Tim flabbergasted. Tim fell backwards onto a bench. "My jam sandwich!" shouted Turvy. But Tim had already sat on it and waved his legs about. Do you know why? The mouse had mistaken Tim's trouser leg for a tube!

At last it was free. Meanwhile several onlookers had gathered. The frog was laughing but you could only hear, "Croak, croak!"

Tim's mother consoled him and washed his trousers. "You might be followed by an army of ants otherwise," teased Turvy.

The race

One day Tim and Turvy were unusually quick at washing and getting dressed. Their mother was quite surprised. Even at breakfast they were quiet for a change. They took their satchels and put their pixie caps on their heads. "Hey, the pink cap is mine!" cried Turvy and grabbed it off Tim's head. Quickly they kissed their mother good-bye and ran outside. On their way to school Turvy whistled a tune, his favourite tune. And many coloured pixie caps appeared from everywhere. "Quick, quick! Turvy is already going to school," cried Toby, as his mother was still fastening his coat. He collected all his school things and ran after the others. Why was it that Tim and Turvy had so many friends? Because they were always such good fun! "Come on, let's race to the school. We'll be there much quicker," suggested Tim. "Great," cried Turvy and lined up next to him. They all joined in. "Ready, steady, go!" and they all ran to school as fast as they could. Who else, do you think, ran with them? You're right, two little rabbits.

On the way to school

One morning four pixies went to school together. Their laughter and shouting could be heard for miles. They set off from home a little earlier so that they could play for a while on the way. "What shall we do? asked Tim. "Let's have a race," suggested Turvy. "Oh no, we always do that!" replied Tim. "How about 'I spy races', then," said Toby. "Oh yes, let's do that!" they all cried as they knew that game well.

It was Toby's turn first. The others took each others hands and danced around him in a circle. "I spy with my little eye something beginning with 'B'." "Butterfly," shouted Tim and he raced towards the

butterfly fluttering along with the pixies. Now it's Tim's turn. "I spy with my little eye something begining with 'D'." "Daisy," shouted Turvy as he raced towards the daisies.

Suddenly the sound of the school bell could be heard through the entire forest. Now the pixies had to hurry. Quick! Quick!

Our four friends grabbed their satchels. And because Toby grabbed too hard, the bag opened and the contents spread out in the grass. "Look what he carries to school!" cried Tim. Besides books and pens they saw a car, two apples, a sausage, a balloon, a roll. And even a cucumber!

Late!

"Look," said Tim, "Isn't that a beautiful flower? It probably was the model for our school bell." They all admired the bluebell and compared it with the school bell. "Why do we only have one bell in the school? It would be much nicer if we had several little bells like the flower," said Turvy.

They decided to race the last part of the way. Today it was Tim's turn to give the starting sign. "Ready, steady, go!" The pixies ran so fast that they nearly lost their caps.

Who do you think was first at the school gate? Today it was Toby. "I'm so fit today because I had two bowls of cereal for breakfast this morning," he said proudly.

"I'll do the same tomorrow and then we'll see!" muttered Turvy to himself.

There was nobody else there yet. Tim knew why. "Look at the clock. We are much too early! Turvy suggested they play in the meadow for a little while. Tim joined in but Terry preferred to stay in the classroom. Tim and Turvy enjoyed their game so much that they didn't hear the bell. When they went back to the school playground it was empty again. Perhaps the lesson had started already? Yes, it had!

The teacher was just writing something on the blackboard. Tim and Turvy tried to sneak quietly to their places when the teacher suddenly turned round. He looked at them over the rim of his glasses. Tim and Turvy were quite ashamed, looked to the ground and whispered, "We didn't hear the bell."

Good friends

Tim and Turvy did their sums very well again today. They knew their two times-table by heart, already. "How do you do it?" asked Toby. "We have thought up a good game," explained Turvy. "We count everything we can think of. One of us says, 'eight eggs' then the other one has to count out: two, four, six, eight. When I call 'twelve strawberries', the other has to count backwards: twelve, ten, eight, six, four, two, nil."

"We always invent new games with numbers. That's great fun," added Tim.

During playtime Tim was looking for his apple. "It was a beautiful apple with bright red skin!" he cried angrily. But what did he see? Trev was biting into his apple with relish. "How dare you eat my apple?" asked Tim, very angrily. "It was lying under my seat and I thought it was mine," replied Trev.

"Come on, let's look for wild strawberries!" said Turvy. A few pixies followed him. In a clearing behind the school stood magnificent red strawberries. Plenty for everyone. Mmm! Delicious! But what was going on there? Two snails were having a race. "That's not a race," said Tim. "That should be called something else!"

Meanwhile as they watched the race the bell rang for the end of playtime. They had to hurry, they didn't want to be late again!

Gymnastics

During playtime Trev's Grandad brought him his sandwiches which he had forgotten. Several pupils gathered around Trev's Grandad. "What do you like best in school?" he asked them. "Playtime, of course!" cried some of them. "And also gymnastic lessons!" said some of the others.

"Hurray, now it's gymnastic time!"

Playtime wasn't quite over yet but the pixies stormed into the changing room. They took off their jackets and changed shoes. And what happened to their tall pixie caps? The little pixies lined up their caps all along the edge of the meadow. Why? Because they looked so funny, eleven tall, multi coloured caps all in a row! That's what the animals thought, too. Merrily the little pupils did head-over-heels, stood on their heads or tried to walk on their hands. Wham! — Toby fell on his back. It wasn't very easy to walk on one's hands! But he tried again and again. He would surely manage it soon. Tim and Terry were leap-frogging. Before every leap Tim cried, "Hoppla!" and Terry nearly fell over because he was laughing so much.

After an hour of gymnastics they had to put their caps back on. Put on their jackets! Change their shoes! "Oh, these silly shoelaces!" grumbled Tim. He couldn't manage to tie them. "Please tie them for me," he asked his brother. "Only if you give me half your piece of cake!"

"Oh, alright then," said Tim. What else could he do?

At home

"I'm ever so hungry!" said Turvy on the way back. Tim agreed, "I feel as if I haven't eaten for two days!" They raced the last part of the way. They both rushed through the gate at the same time. Great! The table was laid in the garden today. "Hello, we're back. And we are very, very hungry!" cried Tim and Turvy.

They quickly took their satchels into the house and washed their hands. They sat next to their father and looked expectantly at the soup tureen which their mother was just carrying out. Mmm, the soup smelled delicious!

Later as they started to eat their cake, Turvy kicked his brother's leg. "Shoelaces! Cake!" he whispered behind his hand. But their mother heard and asked, "What kind of cake is that?" But Tim and Turvy only giggled.

Later they did their homework. They started with the essay. "That would be fun if we had to write an essay every day for homework!" said Tim.

"Yes, and then we could write what happened each day. Something exciting every day!" added Turvy.

Dreams

After doing their homework Tim and Turvy usually had enough time to play. They raced through the forest and meadow with their friends. They were tired but happy when they returned home in the evening.

Before they went to bed they told their parents what happened during the day. "The teacher was pleased with us because we did very well at sums and writing essays," they told them proudly.

"I helped a beetle. It had fallen on its back and I put it on its legs," said Tim.

And I found a new place with juicy strawberries," remembered Turvy.

Soon the little pixies were lying peacefully in bed. Their eyes closed and they were asleep. Tim and Turvy met their friends by the swing. One was swinging so high that he lost his tall cap. The others were rolling in the grass with laughter. That was Tim's dream.

Turvy dreamed of a large plate of cake that he was allowed to eat all by himself. He kept an an eye open so that Tim wasn't sneaking in.

Meanwhile he was eating heartily. "Ow, ow, my stomach!" Mother was right when she said, "Too much is bad for you!" Turvy woke up and was glad that it was only a dream. Soon he slept peacefully again.
Good Old Moon looked through the window and smiled at the two pixies.

Last day at school

"Last day at school!" cried Tim and Turvy while they were still in bed. In the bathroom, too, they behaved quite wildly. Before Tim realized Turvy had smeared some toothpaste onto his nose. "You just wait!" At breakfast Turvy nearly knocked his cocoa all over the table. His father said, "You are really ready for your holidays. I'm glad school is finished for a while." Tim and Turvy were a little ashamed. In the afternoon they came home with their school reports. Great joy for everyone! The children were happy about their good marks.

In the evening they had a lovely torchlight parade. All the children from the neighbourhood went along with their little lanterns. Tim even made up a little poem: "With lanternlight we walk along
our lights are shining bright.
Like the stars in the sky we walk along,
we are pixies in the night."
And they all sang, "We are pixies in the night, lalala!"

Tit for tat

Penny and Gina were usually very good friends. Sometimes, however, they fought so much, they were like two wild beasts.

One day the girls went to the fun fair with their mothers. Each of the girls bought a beautiful gas-filled balloon. When they went home their mothers were having a cup of coffee and chatting in front of the house, while Penny and Gina played in the garden.

But then Penny's balloon got caught in a rosebush. Bang! It had burst and only a few bits of rubber remained on the string. Penny was quite upset. But Gina had no pity. Now, as only she had a balloon, it was extra special and she took great care of it. She tied it to the handlebars of her tricycle so it wouldn't fly away. Penny watched her. "All balloons burst eventually, even yours!" she kept saying. "Mine won't," said Gina triumphantly. "I will take extra care and look after it!" And she dashed off on her tricycle through the flowerbeds. Crash! Her tricycle toppled over. The string of the balloon slipped off the handlebar and it flew higher and higher into the air. Gina lay on the ground and watched it disappear. Penny laughed. Now both balloons had gone and soon peace was restored.

Conversations in the hall

Peter had taken off his wellies and placed them with the other shoes. He had just been outside where he had stepped through some magnificent muddy puddles. The shoes were neatly lined up, when they suddenly came alive.

"It's a disgrace," said a new pair of shoes angrily, and tried to push away from their neighbours, those wet and muddy wellies. The wellies stood in a large, brown puddle and laughed heartily. And a little stream of muddy water got closer and closer to the other shoes. They anxiously huddled together. They were very upset, they straightened their smooth leather, turned up their noses and didn't speak another word.

"Look at those arrogant shoes!" said the left wellie to the right one. "We are Peter's favourites, not those posh 'walking shoes'. You can't even step into a puddle with them!"

The rest of the shoes became more and more angry. But then Peter came in again. He went straight to the wellies, slipped into them and strode off for new adventures. The other shoes had to stay behind and to make matters worse they were left in a nasty brown puddle!

In the woods

"If the weather is nice on Sunday we'll drive into the woods," said Jimmy's father. But Jimmy wasn't at all pleased about it. "Oh, on Sunday Tommy and I were going to fly my new kite," he complained. "You can fly your kite on Monday afternoon when you've finished your homework," said his father.

On Sunday — right after lunch — his father took the car from the garage and they drove out of town. Father parked the car on a path near the woods. "Everybody out!" he said, and took some paperbags out of the glove compartment. "What are those bags for?" asked Jimmy curiously. His mother laughed and said, "Your Dad is an old collector." "What do you collect, Dad?" asked Jimmy.

"Well, whatever I find." said his father. "Moss and pinecones to make things with, grasses and roots for Mummy to make flower arrangements."

"Can I collect with you?" asked Jimmy eagerly. His father smiled. At the end of the afternoon Jimmy carried a bag filled to bursting. "That's not all for you, Dad," he said, "You know, I've collected a lot of things that I could use. Tommy will be surprised when I show him!"

"Did you enjoy your excursion into the woods?" asked his mother. "It was super!" said Jimmy happily.

The little sister

Barbara was nine years old and she had a baby sister called Lucy, who was very naughty. Barbara was often in trouble because of what her sister did. This upset Barbara as she would be told off by her mummy, but Lucy would be forgiven. Barbara tried to help her mummy, she went shopping and watered the plants, and helped to bath Lucy and get her ready for bed. She even helped to feed her little sister and very often Barbara ended up with most of the food all over herself, instead of in Lucy's mouth!

One day, when Barbara had come home from school, the family decided to visit Grandma. Barbara was pushing Lucy in her pram and they all stopped at a sweet shop to buy some chocolates for Grandma. The childrens' mother went into the shop and left Barbara to look after her little sister in the pram. Lucy jumped up and down and made a lot of fuss because her mother had gone into the shop without her. Poor Barbara was getting very worried because she thought Lucy would fall out of her pram and bump her head. Barbara started to cry, and passers-by were very concerned about the two children. When their mother returned, she asked Barbara what had happened. The girl explained that she was worried that Lucy would fall out of her pram, and everyone would think it was her fault.

Barbara's mummy gave her a big cuddle when they arrived at Grandma's house, and thanked her for looking after the naughty Lucy so well.

Arthur the garden gnome

In the middle of a beautiful old garden stood Arthur, the garden gnome. He looked really smart with his red gnome cap, little blue jacket and black trousers.

As far as the gardener could remember Arthur had always stood under the lilac trees. There was only one occasion when he had moved.

At midnight, when the church clock struck twelve, Arthur came alive. Then he had exactly one hour to walk around the garden. He could do head-over-heels, swim in the pond or listen to the radio in the garden shed. But at the stroke of one, the magic was over and he had to be back in his usual place under the lilac trees.

One night something terrible happened. Just as Arthur was jumping up and down on the garden swing, he caught his smart black trousers on a splinter. He pulled and tugged until it went 'rip' and the trousers were torn. Meanwhile the clock struck one. Arthur the garden gnome couldn't move anymore. The next morning the gardener had no idea how the garden gnome had arrived on the swing. Arthur was moved back under the lilac trees but luckily nobody saw the tear in his trousers!

The impossible crocodile

A crocodile lay lazily at the edge of a small lake. His friend, the elephant sat next to him on the shore. The crocodile yawned heartily and said, "I'm so tired. I can't play with you today!" He turned onto his other side and closed his eyes.

"I think you eat too much," said the elephant who was very disappointed. The crocodile gave his friend an offended look. The elephant lifted his trunk and pinched the crocodile's side. "You are too fat everywhere!" he said.

"But I only eat a little now. If I eat any less, I'll starve!" replied the crocodile. The elephant shook his head angrily.

A little monkey was watching them from a tree. He was just enjoying a ripe banana when the crocodile noticed him. Longingly he asked the monkey, "Can I have a bite of your banana?"

"Oh, no," cried the shocked elephant, "since when do crocodiles eat bananas?" By now the monkey had only the empty banana skin in his hand. The crocodile said to his friend, "Next week I will definitely eat less. That's why I have to eat more this week!"

The little birch tree

In a park stood a little birch tree with tender green leaves. But the birch didn't want green leaves, it wanted something special. It whispered in the wind one day, "I wish nothing more than to have golden leaves!"

As soon as the birch had spoken its wish, the green of its leaves started to change. When the sun shone onto the little birch tree it glistened like purest gold.

A passer-by was amazed and touched the golden leaves. Then he picked some and put them in his pockets. "This is a disgrace," said the little birch angrily but it couldn't do anything about it. Soon, more and more people came from all over the country. They all wanted to have at least one of the golden leaves. And after a while it stood there without any leaves at all, just like in the autumn.

"Why did I have to have golden leaves?" moaned the birch tree and was very unhappy. But the wind heard the sorrow of the little birch and swung it gently to and fro. And one day, as the sun shone onto the little birch tree, the first tender green leaves started to show on the bare branches again.

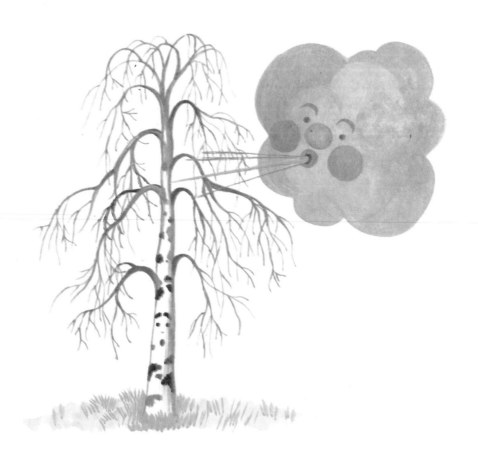

The grasshopper

It was a beautiful, warm, summer evening. The grasshopper took out his violin and sat on a stone at the edge of a stream. After he had tuned his instrument he started to play. It was a slow, lovely melody. As soon as the music started it became very quiet in the forest. The animals gathered around the little musician and listened intently. Every evening the grasshopper gave his little concert, and peace and quiet came over the forest.

But one night no music could be heard and none of the animal's knew why the little grasshopper had suddenly disappeared. However, the hedgehog had watched a little boy catch the grasshopper and put him in a large dark box. The animals left the forest and followed the hedgehog to the house where the little boy lived. The box stood on the windowsill. The sad grasshopper sat inside and didn't want to play on his violin anymore. He missed the forest and the other animals.

Quietly the fox crept into the house and freed the grasshopper from his prison. He jumped on the fox's back and rode out of the door. Then they and their friends returned to the forest. There the grasshopper played on his violin until the early morning. He was so very happy that he played better than ever and all the animals listened admiringly.

The impatient raindrop

Because it was autumn the golden leaves fell off the trees as if they were dancing. Up in the sky a round grey cloud sailed along. It went on its way very slowly because it was heavy with raindrops.

"What a boring journey this is," moaned a raindrop, "I'd hoped to be in the mountains by now!"

"Oh, stop it," said the cloud angrily, "I have to carry such a lot of raindrops today that I can't go any faster!" The impatient raindrop cried, "Oh, don't make excuses! I'll ask the wind to blow a bit harder." "Don't you dare," said the cloud, "the wind is so icy today that you'll freeze!"

"Let's see about that," insisted the raindrop and it went to look for the wind.

But before the raindrop knew what had happened, the cloud simply let it go. The cloud hadn't much time for such rebellious fellows. "Stop!" cried the raindrop, "We haven't reached the mountains yet." But the cloud didn't hear it. The wind heard though. Quick as a flash the wind blew some icy air and the raindrop felt it go right through him. The rain froze and soon turned into hundreds of tiny crystals. The raindrop had become a snowflake that slowly floated down to earth. "Look," said Tommy to his little sister, "it's started to snow already!"

Cherries as big as pumpkins

It was a hot summers day. Timothy had been walking for a long while. Tired and hot, he sat down to rest under a cherry tree. He took off his shoes and socks and leaned against the tree trunk. "Ah, that's good!" he sighed.

Then he saw the ripe red cherries that hung temptingly above his head. "If only the cherries were as big as pumpkins," Timothy thought, "I wouldn't have to work so hard to pick up a few cherries. I could just bite into one giant cherry." While Timothy was still thinking about this, the cherries started to grow into giant fruit. He was just going to pick one when he heard a rustling noise in the tree. Then a giant cherry, as big as a pumpkin, fell on Timothy's foot. He hopped around in pain and rubbed his foot. It wasn't such a good idea after all! Limping and angry he set off for home. But when he turned round again, he saw that small sweet red cherries grew on the tree again.

The little hen that went exploring

Henny lived on a big farm with lots of other hens. They cackled and scratched for seeds, layed eggs and at night they all sat happily in the hen house and slept until morning.

"How boring!" cackled Henny one day. "I am tired of laying eggs. We always talk about the same things. We never see a new face. I want to travel and see new places and people."

The next day Henny set off. She came across a family of ducks. "Come swimming with us," they said in a friendly way. But Henny couldn't swim.

Shortly afterwards she met a cat. "Meeow", it said kindly, "would you like to catch mice with me?" But Henny didn't like mice. "Woof, Woof!" A large dog stood looking at her. "I've hidden a bone. Come on, let's dig for it." But Henny didn't like bones.

She liked scratching for seeds best. "Nobody understands me in foreign places," sighed Henny, "I'll go home where I belong."

That's where Henny lives again. She cackles and scratches for seeds. She lays plenty of eggs. And at night she sits with the other hens in the hen house and is very content with her life.

Nina's dream house

"Good night, Nina," said her mother and closed her bedroom door. "Good night," answered Nina. She turned over and closed her eyes. She liked that moment very much. In her imagination she went out into the garden and there stood her dream house.

She opened the door and at once she was in a wonderful fairy tale world. Here she was a princess. Sometimes she lived on a farm and rode her own pony over the fields. In her dream house Nina had the most wonderful adventures.

But then Nina's father found a job in a different town and the family had to move. Nina felt very sad. What would happen to her dream house?

And then she spent her first night in the new home. "Good night, Nina," said her mother, "and have a nice dream. The first dream in a new home usually comes true!" Nina closed her eyes — and there it was, her dream house. Nina opened the familiar door and went in. She was back in her fairy tale world.

The mole and the anemone

The narrow path went round a bend where a young and tender anemone grew. It was a nice, sunny place. People went by, children jumped about, and often dogs ran to and fro.

On a peaceful summer day Murdoch the Mole passed by. "Super area," he thought, "good place to live." And soon he swung his big shovel hands and dug enormous hills. After a few hours Murdoch had dug a long tunnel and reappeared on the other side.

Then he heard a tiny voice, "Oh dear, he's digging all my soil away and I've no food for my roots," it cried. Murdoch the Mole couldn't believe his ears.

"Who's talking?" he said and cocked his head to hear better.

"It's me, the anemone," she whispered. Murdoch the Mole shuffled across his mole hill.

"Don't be angry," he mumbled into his velvety coat, "I didn't mean any harm. I'll soon fix this again."

He quickly disappeared into the ground and not long after, the anemone could feel soil around her roots again. Thankfully she opened all her beautiful petals and everyone was delighted. And so was Murdoch the Mole, of course.

Nick at the dentist

Nick's mother got very upset with him. He didn't like to brush his teeth. Sometimes he said he didn't like the toothpaste, another time his toothbrush was too hard, yet another time it was too soft. He always found an excuse to get out of brushing his teeth.

"If you don't brush your teeth you'll get holes in them and the dentist will have to put fillings in them. That hurts!" warned his mother again and again. But Nick just said, "Oh, my teeth won't get holes!" and still he didn't brush his teeth.

One night Nick asked for something sweet before bedtime. "Only if you brush your teeth afterwards," said his mother. Nick promised. Then he enjoyed a lovely chocolate biscuit — but again he forgot to brush his teeth!

During the night Nick woke up because he had a bad toothache. The pain didn't stop so his mother took him to the dentist in the morning. He looked at Nick's teeth with a small mirror, knocked at some of them and finally poked about with a little pointed stick. He took out a small piece of almond from between two teeth. "What have we here?" he said, "That looks like a piece of almond. Who didn't brush his teeth, then?" Nick blushed and said nothing. Afterwards, however, he promised his mother that he'd brush his teeth after every meal and at least three times a day from now on.

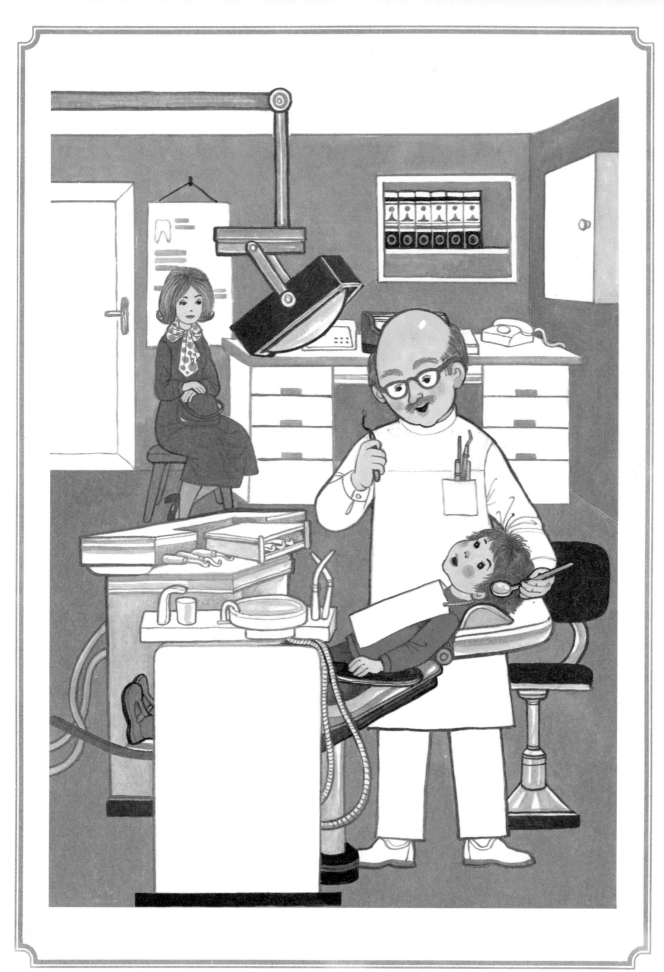

Rudie the rabbit

Once there was a little rabbit. In the summer he slept under the juniper bush and in the winter he had a cosy bed of hay in the wood shed behind the hen house. The hens and the cockerel knew him well.

But the little rabbit didn't like the hens or the cockerel much. The loud cackling and crowing annoyed him. If the "cackle, cackle" and "cock-a-doodle-doo" became too loud he ran amongst the hens quickly, zig-zagging and jumping in all directions. They called him Rudie because he was so rude.

"I'm not a Rudie! I'm a little rabbit," he cried and let his ears flop. "Cackle, cackle," said a big brown hen, "you are very naughty. Why do you have to jump about amongst us so wildly. We get dirty and have to wash ourselves for hours."

"Well," said the rabbit, "Sometimes you make such a lot of noise that it makes me very angry."

"From now on," promised the cockerel, "I will crow only once in the mornings and in the evenings."

"And we will cackle very quietly when we've laid an egg," said the hens.

"Then I won't run about amongst you anymore and you needn't call me Rudie!" said the rabbit.

The story of Blowy

There was once a little pixie who was called Blowy because he could blow into things until they were very big. One day at about lunchtime, Blowy sat on a windowsill and looked into a room. He saw a large plate of dumplings standing steaming on the table. And, because he just hadn't anything better to do, he jumped onto the table, crawled into one of the dumplings and blew into it until it doubled in size. Two children rushed into the room and climbed onto the chairs. "What a big dumpling," said the fatter child, and without waiting she stuck her fork into the large dumpling. At that moment it went "phttt" and shrank because the air had been let out. The child looked puzzled and her sister laughed, "That comes from always taking the biggest one!"

Then their mother brought in two red jellies with custard and whipped cream. Blowy slipped into one of the jellies and . . . blew it up to twice its original size. The fat child immediately reached for the giant jelly. "Splash!" The red jelly collapsed. The custard spread all over the place and whipped cream splashed onto the greedy child.

She learnt her lesson that time. She won't be greedy again and always take the biggest. Blowy was really a very good little pixie.

106

Happiness

Edward the bear met a beautiful fairy-queen. She granted him three wishes. Edward remembered fairy stories where people had wished for the silliest things. But he would think of something sensible!

So he wished that the fairy-queen would stay with him. Then he wished to always be happy, and his third wish was to live forever.

Every day the fairy-queen fulfilled Edward's wishes and at the beginning he thought it was very nice. But soon he grew tired of always feeling the same. One day he became really angry, "That is not happiness," he cried. "I've got everything but I can't be pleased about it anymore." "Happiness," said the fairy-queen, "happiness is something inside you. You have to find it yourself! With every bit of happiness comes a little bit of unhappiness!"

"Then, please, grant me one last wish." said Edward. "Let me live as I did before!" And from then on Edward lived like any other bear. Sometimes he was unhappy, but mostly he was happy. And he learnt that with every bit of happiness belongs a little bit of unhappiness.

The bird and the cactus

A lonely little cactus stood in the desert. Occasionally some camels passed.

One day, around noon, when the sun was burning down without mercy, something soft suddenly fell onto the dozing cactus. A little voice peeped, "Ow, you're very prickly, that hurts!"

The cactus was surprised when he saw a little bird. "How did you get here? What is a little bird like you doing in the desert?" asked the cactus.

"I'm afraid I'm lost!" said the tired bird. "I'm on my way to a warmer climate. In the summer I live in England but in the winter I fly to Africa. But here in the desert I'll die of thirst."

The little bird lay down exhausted in the sand. The cactus gave a little shade so the bird could rest for a while. When it became cooler in the evening, the little bird woke up. "I store water inside me," said the cactus. "If you like, you can have a drink. But you must leave the desert as quickly as possible to find fresh food!"

The little bird pecked at the cactus and drank. The cactus giggled because he was very ticklish at that spot.

When the bird's strength was restored it was very grateful and said good-bye to the cactus.

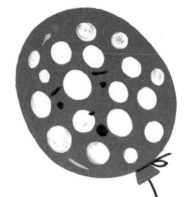

The old-fashioned balloons

At the fairground there was a stall which sold lovely balloons. Mr. Arnold, the man who sold them, had a whole bunch of strings in his hand to which the balloons were tied.

They were beautiful balloons, bobbing gently on the strings. Mr. Arnold knew how to keep them moving with a flick of his wrist. This looked very funny! It was as if some balloons tried to get to the front to be seen better. There were small and large heart-shaped balloons in many colours, some had nice pictures on them. Others looked like bunnies. Many of the balloons had flowers or faces painted on them. But two balloons were simply round and red with big white spots.

"Ha," said one of the heart-shaped balloons, "look at those two round red ones, who'd want them? Ordinary white spots, that's really old-fashioned!"

The two big red balloons with the white spots became very sad when they heard the heart-shaped balloons talking about them.

Then two children with their father ran towards the bobbing balloons. They went straight to Mr. Arnold. The boy pointed to the big heart-shaped balloons but the girl shook her head and said, "No, all the other children have those balloons. Look at these pretty ones with the white spots, they look lovely."

"You're right, let's have those," said the boy happily.

And that's how the old-fashioned big red balloons with the white spots were sold first. They were really happy then!

Judy and the pea

Little Judy was a very energetic little girl. She ran and jumped and climbed, skipped and dashed about all day long. In the evening everybody else
was very, very tired — her father, mother and her grandma. However,
Judy was wide awake, even in bed. Usually she fell asleep sitting up and
her mother lay her down. But Judy carried on moving and kicking even
during the night.

One day when Judy was playing in the kitchen she found a pea. She
rolled it backwards and forwards like a marble and then she put the pea
into her nose. Just to see if it fitted! But she couldn't get it out again! She
tried to poke it out with her little finger — it just went in deeper and
deeper. She got frightened and started to cry. Then she screamed and
howled.

Her mother and father and grandma rushed in. They all tried to get the
pea out of Judy's nose. One pushed, the other pulled and the third poked.
But nothing worked. And the more Judy cried, the more the pea swelled
up.

Then her mother took Judy to the doctor. He shook his head when he
saw Judy. He took the pea out of her nose with a tiny little pair of
pincers.

Everyone was very relieved, especially Judy. She promised she would
never do a silly thing like that again.

Jack is not hungry

"Jack, come on in for your lunch!" said his mother, but he wasn't hungry. Jack was never hungry. He ate his food so that his mummy didn't get angry. "Jack," said his father during lunch, "How would you like to stay with your friend Robert for a few days? Grandma is ill so Mummy is going to visit her for a while."

"I'd loved to," said Jack. "I like it at Robert's house, there are always so many children to play with. Is Grandma going to be alright?"

"Of course," said Daddy. Next day they went to Robert's house. He was playing in the garden with his brother and sisters. Jack couldn't wait to join in so he hardly noticed when his mother left.

"Come in, everybody, it's lunchtime," called Robert's mother after a while. Robert and his brother and sisters immediately left all the toys, and stormed into the house. Jack was a bit surprised — and then he followed them. He sat at the table and ate up everything just like the others.

When his mother returned from Grandma's, she saw Jack's lovely round, rosy cheeks. "I just need some brothers and sisters," said Jack, "then I'll enjoy eating much more!"

The curious mouse

A little stream ran merrily between meadows and under trees. To the left and right of its banks, lovely round elder bushes grew. Under one of them lived a little mouse. Every day it scurried through the grass, ran to the stream and jumped over the twigs of the bushes. The little mouse was very, very curious.

One day it sat under the elder bush and nibbled on some berries. Suddenly it saw something red bobbing along in the water. It came closer and closer. "I must have a look," thought the curious mouse, and it ran to the stream as quickly as it could.

But it couldn't see anything because of the tall grass. It stuck its pointed nose into the air. A branch hanging over the water was just the right thing to cling on to. It hopped onto it, climbing higher and higher. A frog sitting at the edge cried, "Careful!" and waved its green arms about. But the mouse didn't listen. Then it saw what the red thing was. It was a doll's suitcase, floating in the water. The mouse was so surprised that it let go of the branch and fell head first. It didn't fall into the water but landed right on the doll's suitcase. "You were lucky there!" said the frog and he helped the mouse out of the water.

The mouse thanked the frog. It also decided that it would try not to be so curious all the time.

The flying elephant

A young elephant was very bored amongst all those large grown-up elephants. He envied the birds that were free to fly in the sky. One day, when nobody noticed, he left the others and ran as fast as he could through the forest and up the nearest hill. Here he decided to learn to fly. He flapped his big ears like sails, blew his trunk like a trumpet into the silence, and, with his four short legs, he jumped down. A lizard which had been sunbathing on a stone saw the large grey shadow coming towards her and just managed to run to safety when the little elephant plopped down next to her. He winced, stood up on his legs and put his tail between his legs.

"A flying elephant, that's the most unusual thing I've ever seen!" said the lizard in amazement.

"Oh be quiet," said the little elephant, "I hurt all over!"

"You should appear in the circus, your flying was really super!" said the lizard.

"I don't want to fly anymore!" cried the little elephant, "I just want to get home to my Mummy!" and he stormed back to the other elephants.

Paul and the pedestrian crossing

Paul was a dreamer, and that worried his parents a lot. It was very dangerous to be dreaming in the busy street!

One day Paul wanted to see his friend Tom. He put his favourite toy goblin under his arm and set off. But because he was dreaming again, he walked straight over the pedestrian crossing without looking left or right. There was a loud screeching noise and Paul got such a fright that he let go of his goblin. He jumped back onto the pavement. A very large lorry had stopped and an angry man stuck his head out of the window. "You must be careful!" he shouted, "you can't go round in a dream in busy traffic!" The driver was angry because he was worried. When he saw that Paul was alright he drove off.

Paul quickly gathered up his little goblin. Oh, it looked terrible! All dirty and flattened. Paul went home crying and told his mother what had happened. "Lucky you didn't get knocked over," she said. "We'll fix your goblin again. But you must promise from now on that you will always look right, then left and then right again when you get to a pedestrian crossing." Paul agreed to this and also not to walk around in a dream.

The woodworm

In a room there was a beautiful old clock. It was probably over a hundred years old, and was too proud to talk to a simple cupboard or even a chair. One day, as the clock loudly struck four o'clock, a little worm crawled up the wall, straight towards the old clock. He looked for a suitable place to start drilling his holes, when the clock noticed him.

"Don't you dare!" she cried terrified. "I'm the most valuable piece in the room! It's bad enough that I have to talk to you at all."

But the woodworm didn't pay any attention, he crawled across the face of the clock to find the best spot.

"I've been in the dining room of a king and nobody was allowed to touch me! Only the king himself could move my hands!" said the clock, trying to stop the woodworm. But at last the woodworm had found a good spot and started to drill straight into the wood. He said, "I don't care about any king!" And quietly he drilled deeper and deeper.

124

The little red hat

Rosemary had a little red hat. It was decorated with a blue ribbon and a bunch of forget-me-nots.

On a summers afternoon Rosemary's grandma said, "Let's go raspberry picking." Rosemary put on her little hat, took her basket and they went to the woods behind the house. They picked lots of raspberries until Rosemary cried, "My basket is full!" and she threw her hat up in the air. But — oh dear — it didn't come back down. They looked for the hat until darkness came. But the little hat didn't turn up. Rosemary was very sad but her grandma said, "Don't worry. We'll find it again one day."

Summer, autumn and winter passed. As it became spring again Rosemary went to the woods to pick some cowslips. She suddenly noticed some birds chirping noisily. The sound came from a hazelbush. Carefully she moved the branches and . . . there was a bird family nesting in her little red hat! "Please, Rosemary," begged the mother, "Let me have your red hat for a little while longer. Just until my children have left the nest." Rosemary was a kindhearted child and said, "You can keep it. It doesn't fit me anymore." And when the bird children left the nest, they sang a very special song just for Rosemary.

Robin's disturbing night

Robin's mother had asked him to tidy up all his toys before he went to bed. But Robin didn't like tidying up at all, and he was very tired that evening. "Well, you'll see . . ." said his mother. Robin climbed into bed wondering what his mother had meant when she said "you'll see". But he closed his eyes and fell asleep.

In the middle of the night he was woken by a very loud noise. His fire engine drove round the room tooting and ringing, followed by the police car with the loud siren and all the little cars ran about merrily, too. "Ouch, Ouch," said the teddy who lay on the floor, "the fire engine drove right over me!" When the cars started to drive all over his nice books and tear them, Robin became angry. "Stop, stop!" he cried, "Mummy was right! From now on I'll always tidy my toys away in the evening!" Suddenly all was quiet. Robin looked all around the room. It was morning! Did he dream everything? Robin wasn't quite sure. He tidied up his toys every evening, just in case.

Seeds in the ear

Auntie Val had come to help because James and George's mother had to go into hospital. The two boys soon realised that Auntie Val wouldn't put up with any nonsense. "It's no use trying it on with her," said George to his little brother James. George went to school already. He always laughed at James when he tried to escape being washed by his mother.

On the first night Auntie Val noticed that James didn't like water much. She found all sorts of things in his ears! She said, "Oh dear! You could sow seeds in your ears! And during the night green grass will grow out of them!" And she scrubbed so hard with the flannel that James's ears were really red and hot. When James awoke the next morning he found a little daisy flower on his pillow. He showed it to George who grinned and said, "That probably grew out of your ear during the night! And it broke off when you turned onto the other side."

"But Auntie Val really scrubbed my ears hard!" cried James.

"Perhaps there was just a little bit left at the bottom," said George.

"Of course it was George who put the daisy on the pillow," James thought. George wouldn't admit to it. And because James wasn't quite sure if the daisy had grown out of his ear or not, he decided to wash himself thoroughly every day.

Tommy at the Post Office

Tommy was four and a half years old and didn't go to school yet. But he could read quite well already.

One day his mother gave him a little piece of paper and said, "There is a parcel for you from your grandparents at the post office. Go and pick it up."

Tommy was very proud to be asked to do such an important thing and marched off to the post office with the piece of paper. "I hope they will give me the parcel," he thought. "How big was it? What could be in it?" he wondered while he waited. When it was his turn, Tommy pushed the piece of paper over the counter. But he wasn't quite tall enough for the man to see him over the counter. He didn't know who had pushed the piece of paper towards him. He read it and said, "Mr. Tommy Smith, please."

"I'm here," Tommy whispered from below the counter. Astonished, the man leaned over. When he saw the little fellow he laughed and said, "You must be Mr. Tommy Smith. There is a big parcel here addressed to Mr. Tommy Smith." And he handed the parcel to the boy.

Tommy left the post office blushing. Everyone laughed kindly at him. He was very embarrassed because his grandparents had written "Mister" Tommy Smith on the parcel! But he was very pleased with the football that was in the parcel.

Patrick the runaway

"Patrick come in and have your tea," his mother called every night. Patrick usually pulled a face but gathered his toys and went in.

One summer evening, though, Patrick just didn't want to go inside. He ran down the road a little way where his mother couldn't see him. "Patrick, Patrick!" she called but Patrick just carried on playing. His ball rolled down the street and he ran after it. He didn't recognise the houses anymore but he saw a playground. He sat in the sandpit with some other children and started to make lovely sandcastles. Then one mother after another came to pick up her child, until Patrick was the only boy left in the sandpit. He began to feel afraid and ran into the street. He stood and cried because he didn't know his way home.

Luckily his Uncle Jim passed by. "Don't you know your way home, Patrick?" he asked. "Come on, I'll show you." And he took Patrick home. His mother was beginning to get worried and was very relieved when Patrick came home with Uncle Jim.

Of gnomes and people

A little gnome had built his house in a quiet clearing in the woods. It was a peaceful summer afternoon and he sat on a bench in his garden and smoked his pipe. He noticed an unusual humming noise but didn't pay much attention. Suddenly he was disturbed by loud voices.

A family with two children had arrived. They had brought folding chairs, a large picnic basket and even a barbecue. They placed the chairs near the gnome's house and started the barbecue. The children were romping through the woods and a noisy radio could be heard. That was enough for the little gnome. He went back into his house and waited until the family had gone. When he opened his front door he couldn't believe his eyes. His beautiful garden looked like a rubbish tip. Paper plates, paper napkins, empty tins and banana skins, paper cups and tissues were strewn all over his flowerbeds. Sadly the little gnome looked at the mess.

The news of those badly behaved people spread quickly throughout the gnome kingdom. And that's why gnomes always hide when people come near.

The absent-minded pixie

Once upon a time there lived a baker in a town in the valley. Behind the town there was a big dark forest and behind that was a giant mountain. On its peak grew a tall slim fir tree. In the top of the tree lived a little pixie. Three times a week he made the long trip down into the town to buy bread.

And today, as usual, the little pixie went into the baker's shop. The baker was expecting him and passed him the bread he'd ordered. "Why do you always sit on top of the fir tree?" asked the baker. "I thought pixies lived among the roots of trees."

Puzzled, the pixie looked at the baker. Suddenly his face lit up and he said, "You're right! I used to live among the roots of the fir tree. One day a mouse family with many noisy children settled there, too. I moved to the top of the tree to have some peace and quiet. I forgot that I only wanted to stay there for a little while. Good thing you asked me about it. Now I can live down below and don't have to make the long journey from the top." And from then on he lived among the roots of the trees.

Dachsie's secret

Dachsie was a little dachshund and was the forester's best friend. The forester was responsible for the large forest near the town. Dachsie went with the forester on all his walks. He ran beside the forester, or usually a few steps in front to sniff at everything. That's quite normal for a forester's dog, and they enjoy the exercise, too. Sometimes he begged the forester to give him a little ball to play with. He jumped up at the forester twice and tugged with his teeth on his master's coat. The forester understood and asked everytime, "You want the ball, don't you?" Dachsie barked approvingly and the forester took the ball out of his bag. Dachsie romped about the forest with the ball. But what the dog wanted most of all was to run about in the forest on his own. One day he made the decision, he was going to run away from the forester. He took his little ball, jumped over the roots of the trees and played with his ball.

Suddenly the ball disappeared. Where could it be? Dachsie sniffed along the ground. He followed the scent through the roots to a little hole in the ground. Dachsie stuck his nose into it. Funny smell! It smelled a bit of rubber and strongly of — well, he didn't know. Of dogs? No, not really. But a bit like that. Then a black nose appeared, and almost touched his own nose. Dachsie jumped back. Then a small rust coloured animal appeared. A fox! No — two, three, four little foxes! They cautiously made a circle around Dachsie and looked at him carefully. "Why don't you have a bushy tail?" asked one of them. Dachsie didn't answer because he'd just spotted his ball. He tried to grab it but the foxes defended it. Soon they were all enjoying a good game. They became friends. A little fox wanted to play with Dachsie's collar. The dog was very ticklish and it made him laugh. The four foxes joined in the laughter. It was almost dark when Dachsie returned to the forester's house.

"Where have you been all this time?" asked the forester. But Dachsie didn't tell him. He just wagged his tail and said, "Woof, woof." The forester didn't know what the dog meant. Dachsie didn't want to take his master to the foxhole because that was his secret. Nobody must see the foxhole! Dachsie was going there again soon, to play with his new friends.

The wooden round-about

The best time at any fairground is usually in the evening when all the lights go on. Then the fun really starts.

Only in one corner of the fairground there was no fun to be had. An old wooden round-about stood there. The wooden pony, a zebra, a little pig, a sheep, and even a fox turned round and round to the music of an old barrel organ. However, the round-about was quite deserted.

"I could cry," said the pony, "the children always used to enjoy riding on our backs! Now hardly anybody ever comes here." Even the music of the barrel organ sounded sad. The wooden animals almost started to cry. The little pig suddenly said, "We've got to get away from here! Perhaps children that don't normally come to the fairground would like us." The pony agreed, "You're right. Let's not hang around waiting for someone to come to us. Let's go!" But the zebra said cautiously, "We'd better wait until it's all quiet at the fairground." The animals agreed. They felt a little happier now. The last visitor had left. The stall holders closed their stalls and switched off the lights.

At last it was silent at the fairground. The wooden animals jumped off the round-about and ran into the darkness. They wandered about the strange town until they found a house with a big garden. There were little tables and chairs and in the corner stood a tall slide and a see-saw. The pony saw a sign on the house "Children's Home".

"Perhaps there are children here that want to play with us?" the sheep said. And the zebra said, "Let's stay here for a while. The garden looks really nice."

They all were tired from running and they agreed it was a good idea to stay there. But how could they get over the fence? The fox had a good idea, "The pony and zebra can help the others over then they can jump over afterwards." And to show what he meant he climbed onto the pony's back and — hop! — he was on the other side. They all followed his example and soon they were inside the garden. Each animal found a little place to rest and they patiently waited until the morning.

When the children came down into the garden the next morning, they couldn't believe their eyes. They laughed and cheered. The old wooden animals hadn't heard such gaiety for a long time.

Soon they stood freshly painted on a new garden round-about. They are still there, making the children happy and feeling very happy themselves.

The rhubarb leaf

Once upon a time there was a very sad rhubarb leaf. Rhubarb leaves are usually of no use as only the stems are eaten.

When summer came, the rhubarb leaf became so sad that it shrivelled up and its head hung down limply. Perhaps it just needed some rain?

One afternoon dark, heavy clouds appeared in the sky, and it looked as if a thunder storm was coming. There was a flash of lightning, and then the thunder followed.

A butterfly with beautiful, bright wings fluttered towards the rhubarb leaf and settled on its underside. It was still breathless and trembling all over. When it had calmed down it asked shyly, "May I stay here? I'm so afraid of the rain. A single drop can ruin my wings and I wouldn't be able to fly anymore."

"Of course you can," replied the rhubarb leaf, "just find a cosy place!"

"Bzzzz, Bzzzz," a little bee flew by. Its legs were heavy with pollen which it had collected. That's why it couldn't fly very fast and the bee hive was still a long way away! "Can I take shelter under your leaf?" it asked.

"But of course," said the rhubarb leaf, "just take a seat. There's plenty of space."

"Yes, come in here. Then we're both safe," said the butterfly.

The first rain drops started to fall. They saw a little kitten looking for shelter in the garden. "Oh, there's an umbrella!" it cried gladly. The kitten was talking about the rhubarb leaf and quickly jumped underneath it. "Welcome to the umbrella!" cried the rhubarb leaf happily. Only when the bee started to hum a little song, did the kitten realise that it was not the only one under the leaf.

The three of them talked and laughed to pass the time. When the thunder storm was over, they thanked the rhubarb leaf for sheltering them.

How happy and proud the leaf was! It had protected three helpless creatures? Refreshed by the rain, the leaf proudly stood up again. It really enjoyed being able to help someone.

The polar bear and the raccoon

A polar bear and a raccoon lived in a zoo. Their enclosures were next to each other so they could see one another easily. One day the little raccoon asked his big neighbour, "Where do you come from?"

"Where I come from," said the polar bear, "everything is as white as I am. If it isn't snowing, the sky is blue. And if you can see the sea it is lovely and blue. But it's usually covered with thick ice. I come from the north pole."

"How wonderful," said the raccoon. "Everything is white and clean. That's just the place for me. Then I could stop having to wash everything I eat."

"Well," said the polar bear curiously, "and where do you find the water to wash with?"

"I usually live by a stream. Tell me, what do you eat in your country?"

"Fish," said the polar bear and licked his lips, "there are plenty of fish."

"Fish, just fish?" asked the raccoon.

"What else do you need?" asked the polar bear a little annoyed. "Fish is the best!" The little raccoon didn't like the sound of that.

"But, of course," he said, "fish are good. But so are fruit, corn and plants. Have you tried chicken?" No, the polar bear hadn't.

"Do chicken and fruit taste very good?" he asked with interest.

"They are the best!" said the raccoon longingly.

"That can't be right. The best is still fish!" said the polar bear.

"Excuse me, but you can't judge that if you only eat fish," replied the raccoon.

"Look who's talking!" cried the polar bear angrily and stood up to his full height. The raccoon looked very tiny now. But he wasn't lost for words.

The two of them started to argue over which food was the best. They became quite angry with each other and eventually ignored each other. In the evening the keeper arrived with the food. He didn't know anything about the argument between them. He brought a bucketful of fish for the polar bear. He threw one to the bear who caught it cleverly in his mouth. The raccoon was impressed.

Now it was his turn. The keeper brought him fruit, corn-on-the-cob and a fish. First he ate the corn which was delicious. Then he tried the fish. There they were, the two of them, enjoying the fish. They began to laugh about their argument in the afternoon and were friends again.

Cathy's long journey

Cathy was on her own and rather bored. "What should I do?" she thought. She stood in front of her mother's wardrobe and pulled out some interesting things. A giant hat with flowers, a beautiful petticoat with lots of lace, several blouses, an embroidered cape, an elegant umbrella, and her mother's high heeled dancing shoes.

Cathy put the petticoat on, and looked in the mirror. It looked pretty but it was too long. Next she tried on the hat. That looked very chic. "I must put it on so it shows my fringe," she thought.

Then she tried on the blouses. But one was too long, one too big, the third one wasn't the right colour. But Cathy didn't mind. She put on the cape instead. She looked at herself in the mirror and felt quite satisfied. She turned round to see herself better. That wasn't so easy as the petticoat was too long. She had to lift it up at the front. "Oh dear. I forgot the shoes!" she cried, and stepped into her mother's dancing shoes. Two steps forward, one back and then a deep curtsy as she'd seen in a film.

"Not bad! But I must look a bit prettier," she smiled. Something was missing. Lipstick! Where was Mummy's lipstick? A fine lady is always well made up. At last she found her mother's make-up bag with all those lovely colours in it. Cathy took some of each. Then she turned again in front of the mirror. Yes — she really did look fine!

Cathy was planning to go on a journey. She wanted to be admired by others. She didn't quite know where to go, though. Perhaps to Africa? Or to the seaside, or to her friend Betty's house? Hopefully Mummy won't return before Cathy gets back from her journey!

But Mummy came back! She arrived just as Cathy caught her shoe in the long petticoat and fell down. Cathy started to cry. "Silly girl," said her mother, "your skirt is much too long for you," and with her handkerchief she dried Cathy's tears. "Just as I was going on a journey as well," thought Cathy. But she didn't tell her mother about it. The journey just had to wait until next time!

CHRISTMAS IN STORYLAND

The Christmas Mail

It was almost Christmas. Christmas is a very special time for children. Boys and girls everywhere are busy trying to decide what presents they should buy for mothers and fathers, sisters and brothers. Many children write letters to Father Christmas, asking for special presents. In Storyland children write letters, too! But they write to the Angel Princess. She is the Princess of all the Christmas angels. The children in Storyland put their letters on windowsills. The Christmas angels fly from house to house collecting the letters. They mustn't open them yet, otherwise the secrets escape.

The Christmas Angels

The little Christmas angels came from far away and each carried a heavy bag, full of letters. First they emptied them into a large basket, "They won't all fit in!" cried the Angel Princess. "There are so many this year."

Then she sat down to read all the letters. There were many nice letters. But some annoyed the Princess, and she said to the angels, "This boy Freddy wants a train set and a rocking horse, books and cars, bricks and a Jumping Jack, a lorry and a bulldozer, a computer game and a football. Doesn't he realise that there are lots of other children who want presents, too?"

The angels helped to sort the letters. Oh dear, the heavenly workshop was too small! The little angels wouldn't be able to fulfil all the wishes. But the Angel Princess thought of a solution, and said, "You two, you must fly to the gnomes and ask them for help. They are very good at doing woodwork and I'm sure they'll help us." And the two little angels set off to look for the gnomes in the forest.

158

On the way to the gnomes' house

The two angels had to go through the forest which was covered in snow. "I hope the gnomes have time to help us," said one of them.

"Of course they have. They've helped us before. And they enjoy making wooden toys anyway," said the other.

Soon they arrived at the gnomes' house. The roof was covered with a thick blanket of snow and looked very pretty. Two little gnomes looked out of the window and when they saw the angels they waved.

A deer, two rabbits and a squirrel watched the angels. "The gnomes have visitors," whispered the squirrel, and the deer noticed how pleased the two gnomes in the window looked.

One of the gnomes opened the door. "We are worried about the Christmas preparations this year. We've come to ask for your help," said one of the angels. And the other added, "Christmas is near and our workshops are not big enough for all the work. Could you give us a hand with the woodwork?"

The gnomes were very pleased to be asked and one of them said, "We'd love to! We always enjoy helping at Christmas time. Come in!"

Visiting the gnomes

It was very cosy in the gnomes' house. There was a warm fire burning in the stove and the kettle was steaming. It smelled deliciously of herb tea. Soon the little angels forgot how cold it was outside. They took off their wet shoes and socks and hung them on a line above the stove to dry. One of the gnomes had pulled a bench in front of the fire and the angels were warming their feet. One of the angels even opened the door of the stove to get more heat. A gnome warned, "Don't go too near or you'll burn your feet!" Another gnome fetched fresh wood.

"You must be hungry!" said one of the gnomes. And quickly he fetched some bread and jam for the angels. It was wild strawberry jam and was delicious.

The angels left, and the gnomes were very excited. They called their friends and played in the snow. They threw snowballs at each other and made a snowman. But then one of the gnomes said, "We must go and get some Christmas trees." They'd forgotten about all the things they had to do. They quickly set to work. Two were sawing, one felled a tree with an axe, four loaded the trees onto a sledge and two others pulled the heavily-laden sledge to an empty space beside the house. There they unloaded the trees. They had a lot of work to do!

At work

Back inside the house, the gnomes studied the Christmas letters to find out what needed to be done. "I want to make the little horses," cried one gnome.

"And I'm good at making dolls' furniture," said another.

"I want to paint the furniture," said a third gnome. And they chose the job they liked doing best. They knew they would all do a better job if they enjoyed what they were doing. They set to work. It looked like a real carpenter's workshop. The gnomes measured up and sawed, they planed and smoothed, they glued and nailed, and they whistled and hummed. When they sat down at a large table to finish off, the workshop was a little quieter.

"What do you think of my lovely cow?" asked one gnome proudly.

"But it's pink!" replied another.

"That doesn't matter!" They agreed that he should change the colour.

"That's for Polly," said one gnome, "and the horse and rider are for Peter." They remembered the children's names because they had written really nice Christmas letters.

While they were painting, every gnome sang or hummed whatever tune he could think of. The gnome with the pink cow kept on singing "Jingle bells, jingle bells!"

167

Final preparations

"Oh dear," cried one of the gnomes, "we've run out of time. Quickly, wrap up the presents!" They had finished making the toys and now they were cutting ribbons and paper. All the presents were nicely wrapped up. The parcels were piled high.

Then they heard bells outside. "The angels are coming to pick up the presents!" they cried. And they packed the presents into the sledge. That wasn't easy! One gnome brought a parcel that rattled quietly. "The cow that was nearly pink is in there!" cried one gnome. A snowball hit him on the head. That was because he made his friend who had painted the cow feel silly in front of the angels!

"You've done very well. And you wrapped everything so prettily, too!" said one of the angels who carried two lanterns.

"We nearly forgot the Christmas trees," cried one gnome and he came running with one in each hand. When the sledge was loaded up, the angels said good-bye and drove off.

How pretty the little bells sounded. And in the forest they all knew that the next day was Christmas day!

It's Christmas

The little Christmas angels had worked very hard in the heavenly workshops. For weeks they prepared sweets and chocolates, and made dolls and teddies, cars and soft woolly animals. They wanted to make sure there were enough presents for all the children.

On the last day they wrapped up everything. There were parcels on tables and chairs, benches and stools, even the floor was covered with parcels. At last it was Christmas!

The Angel Princess and her helpers flew down to earth. Below them lay the snow covered town, only the lighted windows twinkled in the night. And when the bells stopped chiming at midnight, they visited every house. They mustn't forget a single child.

Children in 'Storyland' get very excited about Christmas, too!!

The surprise

When it was all silent and very late in the night, two little angels went to the gnomes' house. They carried a Christmas tree and some parcels. The angels wanted to thank the gnomes for all the help they'd given.

Very quietly the two angels crept round to the back of the house, and listened. When they were sure they hadn't been seen, they quickly stood the Christmas tree in front of the house and lit the candles. They placed parcels under the tree. Then they rang the doorbell and quickly ran away to hide.

"Who could that be?" said the gnomes. One of them opened the door and he called his friends. What a surprise! They had a Christmas tree and presents just like the children. What fun! They looked around for tracks in the snow to find out who had given them the lovely surprise. But there were none.

The gnomes didn't know that angels don't leave tracks. The angels came out of hiding. They were pleased they had given the gnomes such a lovely surprise. Soon they said good-bye and flew back to heaven.

The gnomes sang merrily and danced around the Christmas tree. Their singing could be heard throughout the forest. One by one the animals came to the gnomes' house to watch the fun. They had never seen such a lovely Christmas tree in the forest.

The crooked little fir tree

Because the gnomes had cut all the Christmas trees from the forest, one lonely little fir tree stood in the clearing. It was much too crooked to be a Christmas tree, and the top had broken off, too.

An angel flew through the forest late at night. She heard the little fir tree crying bitterly. "Why are you crying?" she asked.

"Because nobody wants me," said the fir tree sadly. The angel quickly picked a few hairs from her golden head and hung them like streamers over the branches of the little tree. And she took the large star from her hat and put it right where the top of the tree had broken off. Two blackbirds heard of the little tree's sadness, and they picked red berries from a holly bush and used them to decorate the branches. A glowworm had heard the tree crying, and it brought lots of little lanterns and hung them on the tree. And now the little fir tree was ablaze with light and very, very happy.

After a few days children came into the forest and saw the beautiful tree. "Look at that lovely Christmas tree," they cried. "It's much nicer than ours at home!" What they didn't know was that the golden threads were real angel's hair!

CHRISTMAS WITH THE ANGELS

Look at the time!

St. Peter looked at the calendar. "Goodness," he said, it's almost time. Today is Christmas Eve! We have such a lot to do. Quickly, little angels, wrap up the parcels."

They started work at once. Each angel had been given a stack of letters and wanted to prepare the prettiest parcel. At last all the nice presents were wrapped up, even the sweets and fruit!

"Dear St. Peter. Open the heavenly gates. It's time!" said one of the angels. As the heavy gates opened, the Christmas bells could be heard from far below. The angels unfolded their wings and off they went. Some tumbled and fell, but that didn't matter as long as they held on to their parcels.

George

Children sat at their windows and watched the twinkling lights. Whilst the children looked out of the windows, the angels crept into the houses.

Meanwhile the angels flew into every house where there were children. One flew to George's house. "There's an angel," he whispered, "it just crept into the house. It carried a little tree . . . and many parcels." George beamed. He hardly breathed as he was listening so hard to find out what went on in the room next door.

"What if the angel only brought me a train and a story book! A car would be nice or . . . a ball, a teddy, nice shoes, sweets . . ." He could hardly stop talking. He wanted to have everything he could think of. But his brother laughed, "There won't be anything left for us. And nothing for the other children either!" And his sister added, "Every child would like something for Christmas."

"I didn't think of that," sighed George.

Then they heard the bell tinkling through the house. The children knew what that meant. Very slowly they went into the next room. "Oh!" they cried when they saw the brightly lit Christmas tree. And when George saw his lovely presents he could only whisper, "Thank you, Christmas angel, thank you!"

Michael in the cradle

The youngest angel was allowed to be part of Christmas for the first time. She was very excited. "Good-bye. I'll fly to little Michael. He's still a baby and sleeps in a cradle," she said to St. Peter. Michael was a healthy little boy with bright red cheeks. He lay in his cradle. The little angel played with the little pixie doll which sat by Michael's cot. He woke up and kicked his legs with happiness. He tried to reach up to the angel with his fat little arms. But after a while baby Michael became tired, and he closed his eyes and he fell asleep. The little angel gently covered him up and quietly flew away.

She stopped before a brightly lit window. What a lot to see! Children danced around the Christmas tree and enjoyed their presents. The little angel saw happy faces everywhere. Humming softly she returned to look through the window in Michael's bedroom. He was still sleeping peacefully.

A house full of wishes

The little Christmas angels flew from house to house. They visited every child whether rich or poor, big or small. And they give each child what he or she liked best.

There was a letter in every window of one house where a lot of children lived. And the list of wishes was endless. Two little girls were in a room on the ground floor. One of them liked helping her mother and the angel gave her a broom set. Her sister liked cooking for her family of dolls. She had some dolls dishes, pots and pans.

Above them there was a little girl who enjoyed painting. The angels gave her a colouring book, some paints and brushes. And her brother got some shoes and brightly coloured socks.

The little blonde girl on the top floor was very pleased with a lovely scarf. And the boy, who loved reading very much, sat under the Christmas tree and read fairy tales.

Don't wish for too much

Mary lived with her mother in a little house just outside the town. She liked going to school and was a clever little girl. Mary's letter for the Angel Princess was very long as she enjoyed writing. She could spell words like skates, dolls pram, paint brushes, puzzle book, tights, dolls furniture and many others without making a mistake. When her mother had read the letter she said, "My dear child, your list looks much too long. The Angel Princess is not very rich this year."

Mary was a little disappointed, but when she realised that she was being too greedy, she almost crossed out all her wishes. There was just one she would like: the Christmas tree with baubles, candles, glitter and sweets. And on the top a lovely big star. Mary now worried whether the Angel Princess was able to bring her a tree.

It was almost Christmas and Mary had never been as impatient before. "Will the Angel Princess bring me anything at all?" she asked herself.

And then on Christmas day all was like a dream. A beautiful Christmas tree stood in the middle of the room. On the top was a large golden star, and baubles reflected the light of the candles. She was fascinated by the tree. Only later did she see the presents under the tree. "Are they all for me?" she asked.

"But of course," said her mother. Mary thanked the Christmas angels and then her mother. She hadn't had such a lovely Christmas for a long time.

Back in heaven

The bag of presents was empty now. And all the Christmas angels had returned to heaven. They were very happy. They loved Christmas just as much as the children. For them there was no better Christmas present than seeing the happy faces of children under the Christmas tree. What a wonderful feeling it was to be able to give joy to so many children. Some angels shouted with happiness, others hummed softly to themselves, and some angels even did somersaults. When they arrived at the heavenly gates, St. Peter stood there and asked, "I hope you haven't forgotten anybody? Did you visit every child? Have you done your duty?" The angels were a little taken aback by such stern words. "But St. Peter," said one little angel craftily, "we don't just help the Angel Princess because it's our duty. We enjoy it, too. But if you don't believe us why not look for yourself? You drilled a hole in the door specially!" St. Peter laughed and said, "You just don't have any respect! That was supposed to be secret. Now go to your heavenly beds. You must be terribly tired. Tell me all the details of your earth visit tomorrow." And the angels giggled and were soon asleep.

View through the peephole

As soon as the angels had gone to bed St. Peter went to his peephole in the door. He peered through it and watched down below. First he saw the snow covered forest. In a clearing stood a manger full of hay for the animals. St. Peter was glad to see that the forester had looked after the animals in the forest.

It was lucky that he didn't hear the two little angels giggling as they watched him. One whispered, "I knew he would have a look!" And the other said, "Let him have his fun, too. After all, we had a close look at Christmas on earth!" The first angel agreed and they went back to bed.

Meanwhile St. Peter had a good look around. There was so much to see. He had to admit that the Christmas angels really had done their job well. He was very pleased with them!

Christmas at the forester's house

St. Peter looked curiously all over the forest. He saw a little house with brightly lit windows. How beautiful the Christmas tree looked! The forester's two sons looked so happy. They were playing under the Christmas tree with their new presents.

The Angel Princess had brought them their own forest with trees and animals carved from wood. They played at being foresters like their father. They loved going through the forest to check on the trees as well as the food in the mangers and bird's houses. Now they could play at home with their own animals and forest.

Well done!

Satisfied, St. Peter stepped away from his peephole and turned round. What's that? All the little angels had got up from their heavenly beds and looked hopefully at St. Peter. They couldn't go to sleep until they knew if St. Peter was pleased with their work.

At first St. Peter was angry, "You naughty little angels. I thought you were sleeping in your beds." They looked down ashamed. But one took courage and said, "Dear St. Peter, don't be angry with us. We only wanted to know whether you were satisfied with our work this year." St. Peter had to laugh. "Well," he said, "going by the few things I saw through my peephole, you've done a very good job. Well done, all of you!" That's all the little angels wanted to hear. Now they could go to sleep happily.

Down on earth the lights gradually went out. The children, too, were tired and went to bed.

Another exciting and busy Christmas Day was almost over.